The Waiting Room: A Christian Novel

Christian Youth Faith-Walkers Series

C.Orville McLeish

Published by HCP Book Publishing, 2024.

While every precaution has been taken in the preparation of this book, the publisher assumes no responsibility for errors or omissions, or for damages resulting from the use of the information contained herein.

THE WAITING ROOM: A CHRISTIAN NOVEL

First edition. July 12, 2024.

ISBN: 979-8224050390

Written by C.Orville McLeish.

Table of Contents

To all the youths who choose Jesus above all else.

Chapter 1

All Michael O'Connell wanted was to enjoy his measly cup of Starbucks' finest in peace, enjoying the sights and sounds of downtown Miami. Was that too much to ask? Of course, it was. Especially with this loud Bible thumper standing on an old wooden crate on the street corner across the street.

"No one knows the day nor the hour that the son of man cometh," the preacher bellowed. "We don't know when we will die so we are cautioned to be ready. Are you ready to meet Jesus on the other side?"

Michael rolled his eyes and shifted his café chair away from the small crowd gathering around the loud fool on the orange crate. This preacher man was starting to sound like his mother. Thoughts of his mother prompted him to check the time on his iPhone. He had promised his mother a visit before he headed out of town again.

A motorist, waiting at the stoplight, rolled down his window and heckled the self-righteous Bible thumper.

Michael would have joined the heckler if he himself wasn't a respectable young man.

The preacher took a deep breath and kept yelling. "Today is your day. God said in his word, I stand at the door and knock. If any man hears my voice, harden not your heart. Give your heart to Jesus Christ today before it is too late."

Too late?

Michael looked at his cell phone again. If he didn't catch a cab now, he would be too late to visit his mother. Her nursing home kept strict visiting hours. For the amount he paid them, he should be able to visit anytime he wanted.

He left his morning paper on the table and lifted his arm to hail a cab.

"Young man," the preacher yelled.

Michael froze. Was that nut job preacher looking at him?

"Yes," the preacher continued, "I'm talking to you there with the fancy coffee waiting for a cab. Have you given any thought to where you will spend eternity?"

Michael could not believe it. This man was actually yelling across traffic to him about eternity. The nerve!

He threw propriety out the door and yelled back. "You have nothing better to do with your time."

"Jesus loves you."

That sounded weird to Michael. A strange man telling him that another man loved him.

"Doesn't that sound a little bit gay to you?" he mumbled to himself.

"What was that?" the preacher asked.

"Why don't you get a real job and stop harassing hard working people with your fables."

Thankfully a cab finally pulled up. He happily left the crazy preacher man to his own worthless confused babblings, standing on his box on the corner.

He would meet his just end, Michael was sure of that. Within the hour surely, a policeman would cart him off for disturbing the peace.

Some people were just so blind to the truth.

Thanks to his efficient and well-paid cabbie, Michael arrived at Shady Acres Rest Home in under fifteen minutes. He found his mother reading her Bible, smiling and smoothing the pages with her wrinkled hands.

He sat down in a chair facing her and waited. She continued reading.

He crossed his arm and cleared his throat. His mother kept reading.

Shifting in his chair, he crossed his legs. She finally looked at him.

"Momma, how much time do you spend with that book? An hour, maybe two a day. Another hour talking to someone you have never seen...that's 3 hours wasted on a notion that there is some Supreme Being somewhere."

Giving him one of those never-you-mind smiles of hers, she closed her Bible. "Not a day goes by Michael that I don't pray that God will remove the scales from your eyes so you can see the truth."

"Well maybe you are the one not seeing the truth. You spend so much time at that Church, when all they do is preach about offering and tithes. All they want is money and I hope you are not giving them any of the money I give you every week."

She shook her head. "I know that Jesus is speaking to your heart. I just don't know why you keep resisting Him."

He couldn't take it anymore. Why was his mother so stubborn? Maybe her mind was indeed slipping, like his sister had suggested.

Michael stood up and paced the tiny living room.

"I really hate talking to you sometimes," he said, not caring about the rough tone he used. "We can't have a conversation without you bringing that up and I am getting real tired of hearing it. One day you are going to wake up to the reality that this Jesus and that Bible you love to read is a complete waste of time. It is not real and you will regret that you did not take the time instead to enjoy life as it is."

She reached under a cushion on the couch beside her and pulled out a little brown leather book. He knew what it was before she extended it to him. The tender way she cradled it in her hands like it was a rare relic.

She bowed her head as she spoke. Her words were so soft that Michael thought she was praying to herself, like she often did when he came to visit.

But then he realized she was talking to him. "Please take it, honey."

His heart melted. She was going to cry. Ever since dad died, it killed him to see her cry.

She kept talking. Slowly. Softly. "I know how you feel Michael and I know you can be as defiant and stubborn as your father but you shouldn't draw conclusions without knowing the facts. Can you at least read it?"

"Momma," he whined. He hated it when she begged him like this. It was pathetic and made him feel uncomfortable seeing her so vulnerable.

But when he looked at her. Really looked into her eyes this time. She did not look like she was groveling. There was a calm yet determined resolve to her gaze.

For some odd reason he felt compelled to comply.

"Son, this could be your last chance."

He nodded at his momma and he took the small leather book from her. "Sure."

"Thank you, honey. Always remember, Michael, I love you, but God loves you more. I'll get us some hot tea."

Michael gave her a fake smile and waited until she was puttering around in the kitchen to place the Bible in the trash can under some crumpled tissues.

"And how about some nice tea cookies, Mikey?"

From the kitchen next door, he heard water running, drawers opening and closing.

"Sounds nice, momma. My flight leaves in about three hours. I do leave soon, though. Need to get to the airport early to go through all that security they have nowadays. It's ridiculous."

"Never can be too careful these days," she replied. "You don't want a terrorist hijacking your plane. I pray for you so much when you travel, you know, especially since they flew those planes into the Twin Towers."

As his mother prattled on and on about 9-11, his mind wandered. He thought of how nice it was going to feel to sink his toes into the sand of Punta Cana with the woman he loved sitting beside him. With a flick of his finger, he scrolled through her text messages from last night.

He couldn't help but grin as he read them. She was indeed a naughty girl for sending him these kinds of pictures. Two weeks with her was going to be pure heaven. He was glad he had bought the island, instead of renting it like the real estate agent had suggested.

His mother startled him. He almost dropped his phone.

"Michael, please don't go."

"Momma, it's just for two weeks." He pocketed his phone, hoping his face wasn't red from embarrassment. "I haven't taken a vacation in years."

"I saw how you were reacting as you looked at your phone just now. You're not going to be alone in the Dominican Republic, are you?"

He waved her off. "I'm taking a vacation, momma."

"She's a married woman, isn't she?"

"I am a grown adult."

"Otherwise, you would have brought her to dinner. You would have introduced me to her. You would not be running off like a ..."

She hung her head as she placed the tea tray on the table beside the couch.

"Oh, son. Where did I go wrong with you? I tried to raise you right. Teach you and be an example of Jesus' love for us. Jesus gave His life for you, Michael, and you constantly ignore His call on your life."

"Stop preaching to me, okay. I don't need God. You can believe anything you want, Momma, but this idea of a God is stupid. We are our own gods. We decide our own destiny."

"You're hurting me."

"You're hurting yourself."

Michael stormed to the door. "I will see you in two weeks and I would appreciate it if, from now on, you keep your religious nonsense to yourself. You sound like some kind of sidewalk preacher."

Tears glistened in her eyes as he closed the door between him. He figured she stood there crying after he left. Something in him didn't care.

He deserved some love in this cruel world.

Chapter 2

The security check points at Miami International was hectic and time consuming, as expected. At last, he was able to sink into his seat, remove his suit coat, and get comfortable.

Crossing his arms, he closed his eyes and let his mind wander to the warm sands and hot nights that were going to fill the next two weeks of his life.

"Hello there, mon," said a man nearby. His accent was thick.

The smell of marijuana surrounded Michael. It was strong and made him gag. He opened his eyes and looked for the source of the stench.

A dark-skinned floppy-haired man stood in front of him.

"I said, 'Hello there, mon.' Do you mind if I sit here next to you? The terminal is full of bodies heading out of Miami. This be the only seat left. This one here next to you."

Fighting the urge to cough, Michael shrugged. The man's accent wasn't the only thing that was thick. He found himself wondering how much weed you needed to smoke to smell so bad.

"Sure, have a seat," he told the man and glanced at his Rolex. He would only have to put up with this ragamuffin for about half an hour before they started first class priority boarding.

The shaggy stranger sat down, muttering to himself. Michael closed his eyes and got comfortable again. Calming thoughts of sunny days flooded his thoughts again.

"Bun a fire pan you, mon!" the shabby man beside him yelled out. "It's you, church man."

Michael sat upright like a shot. His seat companion was staring at a man in a clergy collar seated in the row across from them.

"Hello, Kevin," the older man said, addressing the foul smelling man with a smile. "Remember what I told you last week when we talked? Have you thought about it at all? There is a way that seems right unto a man, but in the end it leads to death. Jesus is the only way, young man. I want to invite you to church."

Michael sighed. There was no getting away from this Jesus nonsense today. What was the world coming to?

"You want to know why I don't go to church," Kevin said. "Because you don't live what you preach. On the pulpit is one thing but on the streets is another. Fire!"

Michael chuckled to himself. This Kevin fellow was entertaining. He decided to watch the two men talk. Just to pass the time.

"What will it profit a man to gain the world and lose his soul?"

Is that all you got, preacher man, Michael thought.

Kevin had a zinger of a comeback. "Fire on a Babylon belief system that seeks to enslave the minds of the free."

This was better than watching tennis.

"Jesus is calling you out of darkness into his marvelous light."

"Fire for Jesus. Jesus is just an idea. A white man god. Emperor Haile Selassie is the real king and all you citizens of

Babylon will feel his wrath when him return to lead we the black race back to Africa ... back to Zion."

Michael didn't know who this Haile Selassie was but that lively exchange between the men was laughable. And loud. Others in the terminal had taken notice. Including the TSA officers. One of them had taken up a station near the gate. Another was on a walkie talkie about two hundred feet away.

Kevin shifted in his seat, muttering some fiery words to himself.

A woman covered in a head scarf leaned forward and spoke over an elderly man between them. "Excuse me, sir," she said, was addressing the clergy man.

Michael thought this was rather forward for her. Judging by her dark brown eyes and olive skin, she was Muslim. He didn't think they were supposed to talk to strange men.

But he kept his thoughts to himself. The way his day had been going, anything could happen. Jesus himself could walk off the next plane.

He chuckled to himself at the absurd thought.

The woman spoke again. "There is no god but Allah, sir. Christians believe in three but we believe in one. Jesus was only a messenger. He died on the cross. He was a failure....but where he failed Allah succeeded."

The clergyman didn't answer. He was thumbing through the Bible in his lap. Did he even hear her?

She shifted something in her handbag and went on. "A Son of God could never be a slave or die a criminal's death. There is no such thing as sin or hell and this notion of salvation is arrogance."

Finally the man of the cloth responded. "Jesus is the way, the truth and the life. If you surrender to him and give your lives to him, he will save you from hell."

"Jesus has failed to save anyone. Just as he will fail to save you from the death you pronounce upon yourself."

"I'm willing to die for Jesus."

"I'm willing to die for Allah."

The clergyman shook his head. His eyes were closed but his hands stayed busy smoothing the pages of the Bible he held.

"God is tugging at the heart of someone at this very minute," he said loudly. "He wants to save you. It is no coincidence that you are in the reach of my voice today and you think that you are a mess but God wants to turn that mess into a message."

He leaned forward and addressed the woman on the other side of Kevin. She wore the skimpy clothes of a hooker. No wonder this man of the cloth was attracted to her. What man wouldn't be with all the skin she was revealing? The dress she wore left very little to the imagination.

"He wants to turn your tests into testimonies," the clergyman said to the woman.

Out of the corner of his eye, Michael saw her shaking her head. "Why would God want to have anything to do with me?" She tried unsuccessfully to zip her jacket up to cover her cleavage.

"He loves you. For that very reason He died for you. Jeremiah 1:5. Before I formed you in the womb I knew you...before you were born I set you apart."

The girl was crying now. Her face in her hands. "I am filthy. I used to follow him but ... but I went to the streets. I'm so filthy now."

This was turning into a strange side show. Michael expected to see a TV camera at any moment. Was he on one of those weird reality television sitcoms?

The man of the cloth softened his tone. "Isaiah 66:1. To all who mourn in Israel, he will give a crown of beauty for ashes, a joyous blessing instead of mourning, festive praise instead of despair. In their righteousness, they will be like great oaks that the Lord has planted for his own glory."

The girl was crying in earnest now. "I want to be saved."

"And you can be. Today."

The clergyman knelt before her and took her hands into his. With his head bowed, they spoke in whispers to one another. Michael strained to hear but Kevin's phone rang out with some sort of a Jamaican beat.

Kevin looked at the number displayed on the screen and answered it with an agitated voice. "Junior, mon. Where you been all this time?"

"Ras, I want talk to you about the Lord, mon," came Junior's louder reply. Kevin had put him on speaker phone. "Before you get on that plane, you need to get right. Can I talk to you about Jesus, Kev?"

Great! Michael thought. This has gone from crazy to looney. The clergyman and the young girl was still praying. The Muslim woman was looking on with a pinched expression.

"About Jesus! You got to be kidding I. Keep walking Judas. You is a traitor to the tribe."

"There is another way," Junior went on. "What the Rastafarians believe is a twisted version of the truth and the Bible tells us—"

Kevin cut him off. "Lies. That Christian girl you dating only full up you head with lies. There is only one way and that is through the Emperor of Ethiopia. He stood for peace and love yeah. He is the true and living god, not some fictitious prophet who that book claimed to walk this earth 2000 years ago. Get it right!"

"Selassie is dead. Jesus Christ is Lord."

"There is no God but Selassie and even Jesus Christ will bow to him one day."

Kevin hangs up and stows his phone in his back pocket. "This is madness, mon," he says to Michael. "Jesus talk everywhere you turn. Madness fire!"

The clergyman stood, and handed a handkerchief to the young girl. He was smiling like he had done something worthwhile.

What a freak! Michael wanted to say.

Somebody should do something to stop him.

"Revelation 3:14-22," he said in a soft voice, directing his words to the next woman over. "These are the words of the Amen, the faithful and true witness, the ruler of God's creation."

The woman, much older than the first, smoothed her long blond hair and pointed a finger at him. "Why are you talking to me like that?"

The Muslim girl was shaking her head as she rummaged in her handbag.

"I know your deeds," he said, "That you are neither cold nor hot. I wish you were either one or the other! So, because you are lukewarm—neither hot nor cold—I am about to spit you out of my mouth. You say, 'I am rich; I have acquired wealth and do not need a thing.' But you do not realize that you are wretched, pitiful, poor, blind and naked. I counsel you to buy from me gold refined in the fire, so you can become rich; and white clothes to wear, so you can cover your shameful nakedness; and salve to put on your eyes, so you can see."

She was red in the face by this time. "You should stop right now, sir. I'm going to scream for the security officers. You are disturbing us."

The woman took a long sip from the soft drink her male companion held. She let her slender hands linger on his muscled forearms.

"Those whom I love I rebuke and discipline. So be earnest, and repent. Here I am! I stand at the door and knock. If anyone hears my voice and opens the door, I will come in and eat with him, and he with me. To him who overcomes, I will give the right to sit with me on my throne, just as I overcame and sat down with my Father on his throne. He who has an ear, let him hear what the Spirit says to the churches."

"I asked you to stop."

Michael could tell she was trying to be civil.

"You're talking about me having an ear," she said. "I think you're the one who can't hear. Are you deaf?"

The clergyman took a deep breath. "Maria, I know you are having a hard time dealing with the death of your mother but being with this man is not the solution."

Michael looked at the muscle-bound man beside the blond. He was looking just as uncomfortable as she. Michael felt sorry for him.

"How do you know my name? What right do you have to tell me what to do, how to live?"

The man of the cloth knelt on the floor again. The knees of his black suit were getting ruined from what Michael could see but the man didn't seem to care.

"You are not thinking clearly, Maria," the clergyman said. "You used to follow Christ. You used to try to convince your male friend here to accept Jesus. You should really think about the relationship you profess to have with this Jesus."

"I can't wait to see him to give him a piece of my mind," the blond said.

"You used to help the homeless and feed hungry children in your community."

"You came here to judge me? You don't even know me."

"You are allowing the devil to take something precious away from you, Maria."

"God is the one who took something precious away from me."

"I know it hurt to see your mother die from such a painful death. I like to think that the one who has the power to give life, also has the right to take life."

Maria's tone was still tight but she was not talking as loudly. She had taken the lid off her soft drink. What was she planning to do with that cup? It was full from the way she held it.

The young Muslim woman had slid to the front of her seat. She had pulled the long strap of her handbag across her body. Her right hand held a small black book. A Quran, maybe, Michael thought. Things were really going to go nuts now. A holy war of words. Bible against Quran. He groaned and checked his watch again. Was this plane ever going to board?

"Please leave," Maria said. "I won't be held responsible for what happens next."

"Maria, come back into the fold before it is too late. That's what your mother would want."

"My mother is dead, so go bother somebody who cares."

Maria leaned forward, propelling the cup toward the man of the cloth.

Michael didn't see the splash of carbonated liquid across the man's face and chest because at that very moment, his world ended in a ball of intense violent heat.

Chapter 3

Michael pushed himself to his feet. "Where am I?"

The place was shrouded in shadows but he could make out the others lying around him on the floor. They looked to be in a room, not in the airport terminal anymore.

But how had they gotten here.

Frowning he walked over to where Kevin was sprawled. "Hey!"

He shook Kevin by the shoulder. Kevin shrugged him off.

"Wake up!" Michael shouted. "Hey."

Kevin woke up swinging clenched fists. "JAH!"

The others lying nearby woke up and looked around.

"I feel like I suffering from a serious hangover," Kevin said, holding his head. "But I don't remember drinking no rum last night. Must be the weed."

"Where are we?" Michael asked. "One minute we were in the airport. The next minute we're in this strange room."

"Never mind where we are," Kevin said. "I want to know who you are? For all I know you could be part of a bad dream brought on by I weed."

"I'm not part of your drug-induced dream. I don't know *who* you are. For all I know, you could have kidnapped me and these others for ransom and ..."

"No, I am no kidnapper, mon. And furthermore, you don't ask Rasta who am I. Rasta should be the one to ask who are you?"

"I don't know you." Michael was losing his patience with this character. "I don't know anyone here. Why am I waking up in a room with strangers from the airport? It can only mean that we were all taken from the airport. Something happened there. Something horrific." Michael scratched his head. "If I could only remember."

Kevin ignored Michael and started inspecting their clothes. They are all wearing black. "Is where them clothes here come from. I man don't wear straight black. I have a very bad feeling 'bout this."

The young Muslim woman walked toward Michael and Kevin. "Who are you people?"

"And you?" Michael said. "You were at the airport too. Why is your head covered like that with a black scarf? You look like a terrorist?"

"I am Muslim, not a terrorist."

Kevin chuckled. "Not much difference between the two, daughter."

"My name is Aiza. A name my father gave me. It means noble, if you must know. What is this place? Why are we here? All the people from the airport except that man with the collar. This is very strange."

The other people wander closer.

Kevin snapped his fingers. "Jah know! This must be a dream. A very strange dream."

"Which one of us is dreaming?"

Michael wiped sweat from his brow. They exchange confused looks. No one has an answer for Michael's question. He was getting more annoyed and started pacing.

"I don't like this one bit." Kevin started searching his pockets and found them empty. "Where is the I weed?"

That made Michael wonder about his own possessions. His watch was gone and his pockets were empty as well. "My wallet is missing too. That confirms that we have been kidnapped. The kidnapper must have drugged us and taken all our valuables."

The blond woman from the terminal spoke up. "No keys, no cell phone. Nothing."

"We're being held hostage," Michael exclaimed. The innocence in the woman's eyes is touching. He wanted to reach out and take her in his arms, protect her. The hard exterior she carried at the airport was gone now. "My name is Michael."

She smoothed her hair and offered a weak smile. "My name is Maria. I recognize you two from the airport. We're all from that one group of seats." She glanced around. "Except for that so-called man of the cloth that was harassing us ... what about that girl, that hooker who was crying? She's not here either."

Michael followed her gaze. Maria was wrong. The girl was here but not dressed in black, she looked like a regular person.

He turned to face the entire group. "How come nobody sees the obvious but me? We're being held hostage."

They all stared back blankly except for Kevin, who always seemed to have something to say about everything.

"No, Sherlock," Kevin said, waving his hands like a referee after a foul. "Keep that to yourself. Nobody can take Rasta hostage. Jah would never approve."

"Anyone have a better explanation?" Michael's question was met with silence again. "Let's search around for a way of escape. Quickly before our kidnappers come back."

They began searching around. The semi-darkness and dry miserable heat made it difficult. There were six of them here in this room. Surely together they could find a way out. He started muttering to himself as he searched. Kevin followed him closely like a needy puppy.

"There is no door....no window. Who would build a room without doors and windows?"

"Who would build a room without a bathroom? I don't like how I stomach feel."

"Why do you talk so weird?"

"He is a Jamaican Rastafarian," Aiza explained from across the room. "They speak with their own dialect. In his case he is using I where there should be me and you."

"And that makes sense how?" Michael said.

"Rastafarian is a religion, just like mine," Aiza replied.

Maria drew close. "You are a Muslim?

Aiza nodded. "Yes."

"You were born a Muslim?" Maria asked.

"I was born in Turkey which is a Muslim country but I did not find the truth until I was 20 years old."

Michael scoffed. "You talk as if there is an absolute truth."

"There is," Aiza countered.

"That is what I would expect a Christian to say. The truth is what you are willing to believe."

Aiza shook her head. "There is no God like Allah. That is absolute truth."

Michael shrugged and waved her off. There was no use arguing religion here and now. They all needed to concentrate their collective energies on getting out of this room.

Maria walked beside him. "This place is really creeping me out."

"We've been kidnapped. It's the only thing that makes sense. Our captors will be here any minute. We've got to make plans for our escape while we have the chance."

Maria sighs and looked uncertain. Michael looked around at the others. They didn't seem to be searching as diligently as he was. What was wrong with these people?

Kevin stretched and yawned. "I feel like I was sleeping for a month."

Sleeping.

The word prompted a memory for Michael. As he was waking up, or rather coming to from the effects of whatever knock-out drug they had been exposed to, he had heard something.

He scratched his head, trying to remember. "I think I heard a voice when I was waking up."

"What did it say?" Maria asked.

Michael smiled. He liked having her around, despite the fact that her male friend was here too. She didn't seem interested in him anymore. Michael liked the attention she gave him.

He continued sharing, "It was something about it is appointed unto men to die once and after that some judgment or the other."

"Sounds like a quote from the Bible," Maria said.

"The what?"

"Hebrews 9:27." This response came from the crying hooker from the airport. They all stood in shock, staring back at her.

Finally Michael said, "She speaks."

"Why would we be hearing a voice quoting scriptures?" Maria asked. "And why would you know the scripture, Miss ...?"

"Faith," the young woman said. "My name is Faith. Do you want to know why we are hearing a voice quoting scriptures? It's not because we have been kidnapped as Michael suggests. It is because we are all dead."

Everyone except Faith laughed. Michael realized just how good it feels to let off a little steam, even if it is at Faith's expense. Served her right to have believed that crazy man with the clergy collar in the airport.

Michael sobered as a thought occurred to him. Since the clergyman was not with them, maybe he was their kidnapper. As the thought gelled in his mind, he realized Maria has stopped laughing as well. She looked off into the distance.

Had the heat and darkness gotten to her, he wondered. Curious, he followed her eyes and saw what looked like a video playing on a far wall.

That's strange.

He didn't remember seeing a video screen before. Maria gasped and covered her mouth with her hands.

An older woman appeared on the screen. She was walking through a field of wheat with outstretched hands toward them. The sun was shining. Big puffy clouds were floating by.

It looked like a scene right out of the *Field of Dreams* movie. He really liked that movie and the good times he had watching it with his daddy. But looking at Maria's reaction made his smile vanish.

The woman seemed to be looking right into the room. "Maria," she said. "Is that really you?"

Michael's jaw went slack. Was this really happening? Must be some kind of mind trick from their kidnapper.

Maria was sobbing now. "Yes, Mom."

"I didn't expect to see you so soon, but I'm grateful. I miss you so much."

"Mom. Oh, Mom."

Maria was standing reaching up toward the screen, straining to reach the bottom edge suspended high above the floor.

"I wish I could stay and talk, my dear Maria. I wish I could hold you, but we're not allowed in that room."

The images on the screen began to fade.

"Wait. What's happening? Where are you going? Mom!"

"All your questions will be answered soon, Maria darling."

The screen faded some more.

"Things haven't been the same since you left. Why can't you come to me?

"I'm sorry, Maria," she said.

And the screen went black.

"That was your mom," Michael said. "She could have come to rescue us or tell the authorities of our whereabouts. Something. Why didn't you tell her where we were?"

"My mom's been dead for five years."

Chapter 4

Kevin shrieked like a banshee. "Why is the I seeing dead people?"

"Because we are also dead," Faith maintained.

Another yelp from Kevin as he hugged himself. "I don't remember being dead and I would want to think that I would remember dying."

"You are not supposed to remember," Faith replied. "Psalm 146:4 says, 'When his breath leaves him, he returns to his earth; in that very day his thoughts, plans, and purposes perish.'"

"Lady, you are creeping me out, ok. You're sounding like that clergyman from the airport. Ok, I'll play your creepy Bible game. If I was dead I wouldn't be standing here now would I. There is no life after death. When you dead, you just dead."

"My name is Faith, not lady...and there is life after death, whether you want to believe or not. The fact that you are standing here now is proof."

"Did I ask you for your name?"

"Will you stop being such a dope? We are all strangers who woke up in an empty room. How about we try to figure this thing out together, and hopefully find a way out of here."

"Unity is strength is what I believe," Kevin volunteered.

Kevin's dialect was wearing on Michael's nerves. "Can you please replace the I with a me?"

"Unity is strength is what me believe."

"Ok, that still sounds wrong."

From across the room, Aiza called out. "I feel something strange over here."

"Feel what?"

"It's heat. This entire section of the wall is hot." She motioned to a wide portion of the wall. "Much much hotter than the rest of the room."

Michael could see the sweat glistening on their faces and necks. At least he wasn't the only one sweating like a pig in this god-forsaken place.

Maria moved closer to Aiza. "Something is burning behind this wall."

Maria's male friend joined her and Aiza and began inspecting the wall. "This is going to sound weird," he said, "but it smells like human flesh burning."

What nonsense, Michael thought. This guy is full of it. He was just trying to get close to Maria again.

"How would you know what that smells like?" Michael challenged him.

"I used to be a fireman."

Michael looked at the perfectly groomed muscle man. "Yeah, right. You used to run into burning buildings and rescue people!"

"You sound so proud," Faith said. "He looks strong enough to rescue people."

Leave it to a woman like her to say something like that, Michael thought.

"I have reason to be. Everybody knows who I am," he said.

"Except us. To us you're just this high and mighty dude from the airport that got jacked like the rest of us. Now, you're in here ordering us around."

"Sure, I don't know any of you, but I can tell you that I have accomplished far more than you could ever dream in my life. I made more money that all five of us could spend in this lifetime."

"Thing is, your money, status, education and accomplishments have no value here."

"Listen, Fake ..."

"Faith. My name is Faith."

"Whatever. I don't feel dead, okay. I feel normal, except I just can't seem to remember the last few days of my life."

"Do you remember anything?"

"Yes, I remember buying a plane ticket to spend my vacation in the DR. I can't even remember getting on the plane."

"I remember things too. Like I know I am from Miami. Do dead people remember things?"

"Me live in Palm Beach."

"Please go back to saying I, and aren't you Jamaican?"

"I travel hard, yeah! I is always about my master's business."

"I lived in Panama City," Faith said.

Maria got in her face. "Does the fact that you lived in the city of prostitution say something about you?"

Michael joined her. "Of course it does. In the airport, you had prostitute written all over your face."

"You cannot judge someone by outward appearances."

"Sure you can," Michael said.

He pointed at Maria. "Well respected, law abiding citizen" Maria smiled.

Then he pointed at Aiza, "Terrorist."

Aiza protested with a threatening hand gesture.

Then Michael pointed at Maria's male companion. "Idiot number one."

The man protested with his words. "My name is Marlon and I'm not an idiot. You're the idiot."

Ignoring Marlon, Michael pointed at Kevin. "And idiot number two."

Kevin grabbed at Michael, but Faith held him back.

"He is not worth it," she said.

Grumbling, Kevin wandered away from the group.

Michael was disgusted with the entire group but especially with himself for losing his cool. He needed to maintain his head. This situation was no different from making difficult arguments in court. His behavior had not been very respectable for a man of his stature.

But still, he needed to find out about the people in this holding cell with him. He felt it was key to escaping this hell hole.

He turned back to the Muslim woman. "What about you, Aiza? Where are you from?"

Aiza turned away from him, then knelt down and began mumbling something in another language. It sounded like the sing-song prayers he heard a Muslim man on 60 Minutes praying once.

He ignored her. "I guess that narrows it down. We are somewhere in Florida. Probably taken captive by some terrorist group."

"You can't say that," Maria said. "You don't have proof that there are terrorists in Florida."

"You don't have proof that there are none. In my mind, if there are Muslims in Florida, there are terrorists in Florida."

"None of this is making any sense," Maria replied. "Why are we here? If we have been kidnapped then why haven't we heard from our kidnapper yet?"

Without warning, the video screen appeared again. It was in the same location as before but a different person was coming toward them. It was a man dressed in rags. Instead of clouds and sunshine as a backdrop, the man was surrounded by smoldering rocks.

Aiza stopped chanting and rushed toward the screen. "Rafik!"

"Aiza, my love."

"Where are you, Rafik? Come get me. I'm somewhere near you. I'm sure of it. Or at least I pray so. But nothing is as I was told it would be. I am confused, husband."

"Like she doesn't know for sure," Michael grumbled. "The way I figure it, you and your so-called husband are behind this. Isn't that right, Rafik? Or whatever your name is."

Aiza ignored him. "I need you, dear husband."

"I cannot come, Aiza. It's not allowed here."

"Here? In Miami? What are you saying? I don't understand."

"You must listen to me. It's not allowed here."

Aiza shook her head. She looked really confused. "I was promised that I would be reunited with you as a reward for my sacrifice."

Did Michael hear her correctly? "Sacrifice?"

The others overhearing their conversation seemed perplexed by her choice of words too.

Aiza wiped tears from her face. "I have been looking forward to this day for so long. Everything I have done was so I could be with you, my love. They promised me that I would see you again. Praise be to Allah."

"I wish I could have come back to warn you, Aiza."

"Warn me about what?"

"To make a different choice. Everything we believed was a lie. There are no 72 virgins awaiting us...that part was really disappointing...and there is no reuniting husband and wife. There is only one truth, one way...and we missed it."

"No, no. You are not making any sense, Rafik. Who has fed you these lies?"

Rafik looked over his shoulder. "I have to go. I will see you again soon, Aiza, but it will not be in paradise as we had hoped. We made the wrong choice."

The video screen goes black.

Chapter 5

Aiza wailed. "No! Wait! Rafik!"

Maria moaned. "Oh...my...God. We are really dead!"

"Don't say that," Kevin said.

"Face it people, this is nobody's dream. It's happening for real. Why can't I remember anything other than my mother and my hometown? Marlon says we used to live together but I don't even remember any of that. What's going on here?"

Maria goes on and on, talking louder and louder about their plight. Kevin, Marlon, and Faith join her. They are talking over each other. Aiza began to wail and pray again. Michael moved away from the chaos. There must be some other explanation. Some rational reason for all this.

The appearance of a man in a long white garment stopped Michael in his tracks.

"Who are you?" Michael managed to stammer. "Where did you just come from? There's a door back there?"

Michael looked around the man in white to see if there was any evidence of a door having opened.

Nothing.

"How could this be," Michael muttered.

The man is carrying a large book. He placed it on a pedestal across the room. A pedestal that had not been there before.

"I would like answers," Michael addressed the stranger. "Who are you?"

"I am just the Messenger, Michael O'Connell."

"How do you know my name?"

"On this side of earthly life, there are no secrets."

Maria came forward and addressed the strange man. "Where are we?"

"You are in the waiting room."

"I just want know if I really dead?" Kevin asked.

"Human beings cannot die. You were made to live forever, but, the earthly body you once occupied has returned to the dust...your spirits have returned to God and your soul...is here."

"Body, soul and spirit," Michael interrupted. "You sound just like my mother with her three in one theory."

"It's not just a theory, Michael."

"Are you telling me, that there is life after death?"

"I thought that was already obvious."

"This is stupid. All sensible and well educated people know there is nothing after death."

"If you want to call this nothing, Michael - - be my guest...it's up to you."

"How," Maria asked, "How did we die?"

The Messenger looked at Aiza. "I think Aiza can answer that one. She had a hand in it...if you know what I mean."

Michael turned on her and grabbed her arm. She struggled to get away. "I knew you were a terrorist," he yells. "What is he talking about? What did you do?"

Michael grabbed her other arm and shook her. Faith came to her rescue and pulled her free from Michaels grip.

"Leave her alone," Faith said. "What is done is done."

Kevin can no longer contain his anger. "I be 29 years old. I had me whole life ahead of me. I was not ready to die."

"Death is inevitable," Aiza mumbled.

"Death is also relative. It's an appointment no one can miss," said the Messenger.

Michael pointed at Aiza. "Thanks to this terrorist I was early for mine. Was there some undetectable bomb in the handbag at the airport? Something strapped to your body? Something hidden in that head scarf?"

"It was actually a small yet deadly device hidden in the fake Quran I held."

Michael lunged at her again and Faith pushed him away.

"You were a suicide bomber?" Maria asked.

"Yes."

"More like a suicide whack job," Michael offered.

Maria still couldn't seem to believe it. "A suicide bomber in Florida. What are the odds?"

"Jah know star," Kevin added, furiously scratching his chest. "This too much for Rasta. I need some of the good herbs to calm I nerves."

The Messenger addressed Kevin. "You were created for one purpose and that's to worship God. It is the only desire you can have that will be met in this life. All other desires that you carried over from the former life to this one will go unmet because there is nothing here to satisfy it. That is why you were told to seek first the kingdom of God.

"What is the I trying to say? That I is going to have a desire for herb, but will not get any herb."

"Yes and the alcohol, and the sex, all those cravings and desires will torment you for all eternity because you did not replace it with a hunger and a thirst for righteousness, which is really all you needed."

"No I. Don't tell I that. I must can find some dry bush....I need a smoke."

Kevin started searching the room.

"Why can't we remember much from our lives?" Maria asked.

"You are not supposed to....but don't worry. Everything you have said and done in your entire life has been recorded. It can be played out on the screen, as you have seen twice before."

"Everything?"

"Yes, which is why you must understand the reason for a waiting room. There are millions of rooms like this and only one Jesus so I brought you something to occupy your time."

The Messenger tapped the Bible. "I imagine you must have a lot of questions. This book will tell you where you have been, where you are and where you are going. It's all written right here. Just something for you to do while you wait."

Kevin stopped his frantic search of the room. "Wait for what?"

"To talk with Jesus of course. God meant it when he said every knee must bow and every tongue confess that Jesus Christ is Lord. Everyone gets to stand before Jesus either as your savior or as your judge. No exceptions."

The other five people had walked closer to the podium. Were they really buying this bunch of hocus pocus. Michael couldn't buy in. There had to be some other explanation.

He wandered away from the others, mumbling to himself. "I don't even believe in Jesus."

"Look at it this way, now you get to tell Him personally," the Messenger said.

Michael was shocked. How had the Messenger heard what he said?

"I want to go back," Maria said. There were tears in her eyes.

"Go back where?" the Messenger asked.

"To the life I had. I've heard of people doing that before. They have a near-death experience and ask to go back to have a second chance at life on earth. I want a second chance."

"Life on earth has ceased to exist, Maria. You have been dead for over a thousand years."

Michael interrupted. "That's not possible."

"Time does not exist between your moment of death and the day you are called to give an account, so it's going to feel like just yesterday."

This was either a bad dream or some kind of elaborate scheme. Michael was going to get to the bottom of this if it was the last thing he did.

Money always solved every other issue he had in life. He sized up this Messenger guy. Nice clothes seemed to be his weakness. Money was the solution, he was sure of it.

"Whatever they are paying you for this ridiculous scheme," Michael said to the Messenger. "I will double it. I will even triple it. Just tell us how to get out of this room."

"I feel sorry for you, Michael, for even when the truth stares you dead in the face you still choose to deny it. But not to worry...before this is over, you will call Jesus Lord."

And then as quickly as he arrived, the Messenger left.

Chapter 6

"This is crazy," Michael yelled at the ceiling then addressed the group. "We should not just sit here and do nothing."

"There is nothing we can do," Maria said.

Faith walked over to the podium, which still held the large book.

"It's a Bible," she said, reaching for it.

Michael stopped her. "Maybe we shouldn't touch that."

"Maybe," Faith said, "Just maybe, we should. Maybe, you wouldn't be so confused and ask so many questions if you had read it."

"And maybe, you're crazy. Besides, I hate fiction. I prefer true stories."

Kevin chimed in. "I man love the Psalms and Proverbs. Two books written by the wisest man who ever lived. A Psalm and a spliff a day is I recipe for wisdom."

"If you can't say anything sensible, can you please shut up," Michael said.

"You think is you one know law. I know my constitutional rights. Freedom of speech me say."

Michael was utterly frustrated. Faith opened the Bible.

"I used to read that book every day," Maria said.

"So did I," Faith said. "It is not just about reading. God tells us how we can find our way back to Him, as the first man Adam was. It has to be read, believed and lived."

"I stopped believing when God just stood by with folded arms and allowed my mother to die."

"Death is a part of life...but it is never the end. You should not have given up on God."

"God gave up on me," Maria said, new tears streaming down her cheeks.

"You know that is not true. God never abandons those who love Him."

"For a prostitute, you know a lot about the Bible and God."

"I didn't always sell my body, Maria. I know that this is the book that will judge us after death, which is why it's probably with us in this room right now."

Maria and Faith's conversation had not really interested him much until that last part.

Michael butted in. "What do you mean it will judge us?"

Faith explained. "The Messenger told us that we were created for one purpose and that's to worship God. How we worship God is written in this book. God even came to earth in the likeness of His Son and showed us how, by doing it Himself. The only way to Heaven is to follow in His steps and live the way He lived."

"I confuse by your level of thinking, empress," Kevin said. "Heaven is on earth...God is Mother Nature herself and the only example I should follow is that of Emperor Haile Selassie, ruler and king. He set the true example of peace and love for I to follow."

"We have modified the truth a thousand times to suit our lifestyles, and what we want to believe to make our lives nice and comfortable but it fails to change the real truth.... If our lives don't reflect what is written here in this book....we are dead."

Michael rolled his eyes. "What about 'everyone is entitled to their own belief'?"

"Take a look at where you are Mr. Big Shot and tell me how much of what you believed make any sense." Faith had fire in her eyes when she said that to him.

Kevin gave her a little round of applause. "Empress, you have a point still, but that don't change what I know to be the truth and the truth will always reveal itself to an open mind."

The video screen appeared again. A dirty man appears there; he looked like he hadn't had a bath in years.

"Hey, hey visiting friends and neighbors. Any of you got a smoke or a drink, something, anything?"

There was something familiar about this man. Michael squinted at him. Had he been one of his clients? His talk of a drink made him remember his extreme thirst. His throat hurt to swallow. The heat and darkness seemed to increase by several degrees. Michael rolled up his shirt sleeves and walked closer.

"Paul," Michael said, uncertainty in his voice. "Is that you?"

"How do you know that name, stranger?"

"It's me Michael. I used to have a friend that looked a little like you. Don't you recognize me?"

"Michael? I do remember a Michael. Is that really you, old buddy?"

"Yes."

"You should not be here Michael. You should run. Find a way to escape."

"Tell us how you got in and maybe we could use that passage to get out."

"They call it hell, but it's much worse."

"There is no such place, Paul. Your mind is playing tricks on you."

"I would love it to be so. What torments you more than the demons that are there, is the memory of every single moment we got in life to accept Jesus and turn away. Imagine that. You live your whole life thinking Jesus is not real only to die and find yourself standing in front of Him. How weird is that!"

"We never believed any of that stuff."

"Don't matter what we believed, friend. There is only one truth and one way to abundant life and it's all written in that book you have right there. Everything else leads to death, but not the death we had in mind, but an eternal separation from God."

Paul laughed like a mad man. "Many are called, but few are chosen."

"Are you telling me that a majority of the human race are on their way to hell?"

"Is that so hard to believe friend?"

"Yes and even if what you are saying is true and there is a hell...God is supposed to be loving. Why would He throw us into a lake of fire like my mother has said all her life? That doesn't make any sense."

"That is the part that many people will miss in life. The choice is not His to make, but ours. If you want to go to hell, God ain't gonna stop you man. But if you want to go to heaven, He tells you how to get there. I think they call that a paradox."

"If you love me, you will keep my commandments," came Faith's still small voice from across the room.

Michael had heard that from his mother as well. It irked him to hear it from his mother so long ago. And it felt the same way to hear it from Faith now.

The dull ache behind his eyes was turning into a raging headache. He had to get out of this room.

Paul didn't seem to mind Faith's interjection. "Exactly. Good to know there is at least one sensible person in this room. Listen, if you don't love God, how can you be with Him for all eternity? If you can't praise God on earth, you can't praise him in heaven. If you can't love him on earth, you can't love him in heaven and if you can't obey his words on earth, you can't obey them in heaven. You can't choose sin without choosing the consequences man. It ain't possible."

"Jah know star," Kevin said. "I start feel a little turning in I stomach."

Faith replied, "There are so many Christians sitting in church waiting to die to see if they will go to heaven....but heaven is somewhere you have to reach before you die."

"How did you escape from hell?" Maria asked.

"In truth, I haven't. Enough chatting. I need a smoke...I need a drink, something, anything...before they find me."

"Before who finds you?" Michael asked.

"Horrible things," Paul replied with a tremble. "They dig into your flesh and wrap chains around you so tight it blocks circulation. I hate them. Worst thing is, I can't die." He starts laughing hysterically, "Imagine that. We spend our lives on earth fearing death, only to come here and can't die."

Aiza started her wailing prayer again. "It's not supposed to be like this. I want to die."

"We are already dead, thanks to you," Maria grumbled.

Paul wagged his shaggy head. "Death is relative."

"Why does everybody keep saying that?" Michael asked.

"It's a word we gave to a state of being that concealed the real truth," Paul told him.

"What truth?" he asked.

"That we were made to live forever."

As Paul was speaking, two hideous beings appears carrying chains. They rush up behind him. They grab him and put him in chains. Paul bucked and pulled but nothing would stop them. They dragged him away without a single word.

The video screen goes dark again.

Chapter 7

Aiza's wailing stopped. "I'm not feeling so good," she said.

"Not quite what you had in mind when you blew us up, huh?"

"I thought I had the perfect excuse why God should let me into heaven," Maria said, to no one in particular, "But now I am really genuinely concerned."

Faith wrapped an arm around her. "Our time on earth was given as an opportunity to find our way from the sinful state that we were born in, back to our original place in God, as it would have been, if Adam had not sinned."

"Everything else was a distraction," Maria replied. "The partying, the men, the wild living after my mother died."

"And now we stand to give an account," Faith said.

"Utter rubbish," Kevin said. "This is what I believe yeah. I serve the great Emperor Haile Selassie. I believe is him write the Psalms and the Proverbs and in my world, there is no hell...so none a we have anything to worry about. Simple! Peace and love is what I seek and freedom shall be my prize yeah."

"Allah is the true and merciful God," Aiza said, clearly disagreeing with Kevin.

Michael shook his head at all the religious talk. "Christianity was always the only religion that preaches about the existence of hell and we all know it's a scare tactic and I can bet that some

Christian movement is behind this. We should all just stick to what we know and believe and not be shaken by these people. It's some form of a trick."

"You think this is a trick?" Maria asked.

"This," Michael said, waving his arms about. "This is a bad dream. Any minute now, I'm going to wake up from this narcotics induced state."

Maria wrapped her arms around her and looked to be in pain. "I want it to be just that. Only a bad dream."

"Of course it is, and when you think about it. It's practically the only thing that makes sense, unless you want to believe that men can walk through walls."

"I have been faithful to my king. I work hard for my crown yeah. There is no way, after all that, I is going to be cast into a so-called hell.

"Deliver me from this nightmare, Allah." Aiza started wailing again.

Kevin joined the pity party. "Jah! Rescue I. Fire and brimstone on the generation that seeks to enslave I mind and perplex I spirit. Emancipate yourself from mental slavery, none but ourselves can free our minds."

Faith let Maria go and raised both her arms straight up. "Today is the day we all find out who has been living the truth. If Allah is God, then let him be praised and if Selassie is God, then we have nothing to fear but if Jehovah is God, then prepare to be weighed in the balance."

Suddenly, the room was brighter.

Michael spun around in search of the light source.

He saw a man dressed in sky blue and white garments carrying five books. "Well said, Faith."

Faith bowed at the man's feet.

"My Lord," she exclaimed.

The scene disturbed Michael on a deep level. Who was this man and where had he come from and why did he seem to emanate light?

"One of your clients, Fake?" Michael joked.

They all ignored his comment.

"Rise, my child," the Man said to Faith. "There will be enough time for that later."

A table appeared and the mystery man placed each book there, side by side.

Shaking like a leaf, Maria stepped forward. "Who are you?"

"I wish you didn't have to ask, Maria. You and I were friends once."

"Surely you are not the great Emperor Haile Selassie?" asked the Rastafarian.

"No."

"Are you Allah?" Aiza asked.

"No!"

Michael felt like playing along with this guessing game just to pass the time. "Are you even related to anyone here?"

"In some sense I guess I am. I play multiple roles in your lives. I am the one who created you. When you fell from your original state," he said. "I am the one who died for you. Today, I will be the one to judge you."

The man looked at Kevin and touched the first book on the table. It levitated and opened mid-air. The man seemed to be reading from the floating book for a few minutes.

Kevin quickly fell before the man.

"Jah. King of all kings and Lord of all lords, conquering lion of the tribe of Judea. Have pity on I."

"Why should I, Kevin?"

"I is about peace and love. I never shed innocent blood nor covet what belonged to another man. I dedicated my life to Jah works."

"Is that what you referred to as Jah works? Smoking one spliff after another and verbally abusing and opposing my church?"

"That was I in the earlier stages of my ignorance."

"Before you came to this room you mean."

"You live and you learn is what I always say. I once was blind but now I see that I have been walking in darkness but I ready to set the record straight."

"So am I. Someone once asked Haile Selassie if he was the reincarnation of Jesus Christ as you would want to believe. Do you know how he responded?"

The man handed Kevin a sheet of paper. "Read it for yourself."

Kevin read it aloud. "I had heard of that idea. I also met certain Rastafarians. I told them clearly that 'I am a man,' that 'I am mortal,' and that 'I would be replaced by the oncoming generation, and that they should never make a mistake in assuming or pretending that the human being is emanated to a deity.'"

"So what was it for you, Kevin? Was it the idea that you did not have to spend any money on a barber or was it the ganja?"

Kevin stood in silence.

"Maybe it was the idea that all white people were evil or that somehow you were the reincarnation of God's chosen people Israel. What motivated you to walk such a dark path?"

"I was born a Rasta. I was never exposed to anything else."

"If only that were true."

"Galatians 1:7-9 ...but there be some that trouble you, and would pervert the gospel of Christ. But though we, or an angel from heaven, preach any other gospel unto you than that which we have preached unto you, let him be accursed. As we said before, so say I now again, If any man preach any other gospel unto you than that ye have received, let him be accursed."

"Are you not a God of love?" Kevin protested.

"Did you love me Kevin? I proved my love by dying on the cross and making available opportunity after opportunity so you can turn from your evil ways and serve me...what have you to show. How much did you love me Kevin? It is not my love for you that gets you into the city of light....it is your love for me. Do I even need to check your record of unforgiven sins?"

"So, who I a pray to all this time?"

"Yourself. For there is, was and will always be one God and His name is not Selassie. Depart from my presence."

Out of nowhere, dark figures rush upon Kevin and bind him in chains and dragged him off, screaming.

The suspended book disappears as Kevin's cries fade into the darkness.

Chapter 8

"Aiza, wife of Rafik Al Haleel."

Aiza comes and bows before the man. "Master, I served you well. I just called you by a different name."

"I was given a name above all other names. Why would you call me a different name?"

"I served my master well."

"Yes you did. You gave credit where credit was not due...and the sad thing is, you used to believe in me."

"Yes, I tried the Christian way once," she confessed.

"Well, you had it right the first time. Do you still believe that I am just a man....that Mohammed was sent after me to succeed where I had failed?"

Aiza said nothing.

"I could have saved you from hell, Aiza, and all the promises of a better world in the Bible could have been yours...but like Eve in the Garden of Eden, you allowed yourself to be deceived and like Eve, I must banish you from my presence."

The dark figures came and took Aiza away, just as they had taken Kevin away. Her frantic wails died away as her book disappeared.

The blue and white clad man approached another open book as it levitated before him. "Maria? I have sensed that you've wanted to speak to me for some time now. Here I am, if you still want to give me a piece of your mind."

"I was upset then."

"About what?"

"Why didn't you heal my mother? You didn't have to allow her to die."

"You are upset with me for taking your mother out of suffering, out of a sinful and corrupt world to a better place? Does that seem a tad bit ungrateful to you?"

"I was left alone."

"You chose to be alone. I wanted to comfort you but you completely shut me out of your life, Maria. You were a great Stalwart and together we accomplished much, and could have accomplished even more... but you changed from that....to this..."

The man waved his hand at Marlon. Marlon hung his head in shame.

Then the man kept talking with Maria. "You still went to church, still kept your appointments, did what they asked you to do, sung the songs, read the words, talked the talk but it became a routine and stopped being a relationship. You no longer knew me. You no longer had faith in me."

"I did what I had to do."

"You stopped visiting those in prison and in the hospital. You stopped reading my word, you stopped praying. You stopped partaking of the Lord's Supper and washing of the saints feet. You stopped paying tithes; you no longer fasted; had no respect for authority and pretty much dabbled in all manner of sin...You had a terrible attitude. But then, I wrote you a letter and when you refused to read it, I made sure somebody read it for you. You gave up everything that had any value...and the few things you kept was empty and meaningless."

"I had Marlon. I felt his love more than I felt yours."

"Love never had anything to do with feelings, Maria. I called your name every single day for five years...but you drown out my voice with everything that this world had to offer. Whatsoever things are true, pure, honest, just, lovely and of a good report. Think on these things."

Maria was sobbing heavily. "I messed up, Lord. Living with all those men. Living like there was no tomorrow. The sex, the drugs. And I'm sorry okay. I thought I had a right to be angry. I thought I was justified to walk away."

"The fruit of the Spirit is love, joy, peace, longsuffering, gentleness, goodness, faith, meekness and temperance. Everything you needed to heal and regain strength, but instead you choose fruits of the flesh." He read from the book. "Sexual immorality, impurity, extreme sensuality, idolatry, hostility, bitter conflicts, jealousy, outbursts of anger, lack of unity, dissentions, cliquishness, envying and drunkenness. In the process, you gave up your right to reign with me."

"It never felt wrong ... until now."

"Feeling is a fallen function. You become a slave to it when you find yourself walking in the flesh."

"Is this it? Is this the end?"

"This is the last time you will see me."

"Will I see my mother again?"

"No."

"There is nothing you can do for me?"

"At this point, Maria, No. I am really sorry. I can't tell you how many times my heart has been broken today. There is only one heaven, one Father and One Way. Every other road leads to hell," he pauses and points to the dark figures waiting for her in the corner. The sound of chains rattling breaks the silence.

She began to cry once more.

The Man went on, "It is my desire for all men to be saved but your ability to choose has proven to be both your greatest strength and your greatest weakness. The reality is, many will make it, but most will not....most will choose not to."

"I never believed it would be like this."

"I really enjoyed those moments in your past that we spent together Maria, but it is the final moments of your life on earth that really counts. You have to live in that moment every single day because you don't know when death will come knocking at your door."

Her book closed and vanished like smoke.

"Goodbye, Maria."

The chain bearers came and took her away.

The man pointed at Marlon. "You will meet a similar fate, young man."

Marlon bowed before him and, in seconds, was reduced to a blubbering baby on the floor. Michael was embarrassed for him but then he remembered that it was all a dream.

I will wake up soon, he thought.

The mystery man continued talking to Marlon. "You will be taken away by hell's jailors too. Not because you lived a life of sin with Maria, but because you did not choose me."

"But ... but ..." Marlon stammered. "I saved so many people as a fireman. I put my life on the line."

"You did," the man replied. "I agree, you did sacrifice much in the name of saving lives but you did not accept my free gift of salvation."

He motioned for the dark figures to come in from the shadows. "Goodbye, Marlon."

Marlon's book disappeared as the shadowy jailers dragged him away in chains.

Two books were left. Michael guessed that they were for him and Faith since they were the only two people left.

For a second, Michael's heart skipped a beat.

The radiant man turned to Faith.

Whew!

"Faith, you have been a naughty girl," the man said.

"Yes, my Lord."

"Why did you ignore me all those years?"

"I thought I could find my own way."

"Did you?" he asked.

"No. As a sinner I was feeling around in the dark, grabbing hold of anything I could find. Ended up living a life of lust and prostitution, drugs and alcohol. Eventually living became meaningless and I wanted my life to end."

"I can see all that in your records, but nearing to the end of your book, the words and tone of your life changed."

"I was sitting in an airport terminal one day. A man spoke words of life over me. It was an awesome experience. I sensed at that moment that You took me from the dirt, changed my clothes and gave me a new heart and renewed mind and I have served You ever since."

"Well done, Faith."

"Thank you, my Lord."

"You despised Me most of your life, but in the end, you knew Me. You even recognized Me here?"

Faith was beaming with joy. "From the moment you walked into the room."

"Let me take a look at your record of unforgiven sins."

He opened her book. Even from where he was standing some twenty feet away, Michael could make out the empty pages. The other's books had been full of writing. A listing of their sins, he supposed.

What kind of wacked up dream was this?

He couldn't hold his tongue any longer. "What! Her book is blank."

"There are no record of any past sins."

"You have got to be kidding me."

"I am going to ask you to be quiet, Michael. I will be with you shortly."

The man turned back to Faith. "Faithful servant, enter into my rest. All that I have, all that My Father has given me, I will share with you for all eternity."

The Man allowed Faith to hug him before she walked away smiling. The wall in front of her opened up like a tear in a curtain from top to bottom. Cool fresh air rushed toward him from the opening and he saw blue sky, clouds, and the glistening green leaves of a tree.

He took a stumbling step toward the scene in the wall. One minute Michael saw her walking off into the wonderful scene in the wall, the next minute she was gone. Like a ghost or something.

The stifling heat and darkness returned just as quickly. The pain in his head, now a full-blown migraine, made it next to impossible to keep his eyes focused on the Man standing in front of him.

He couldn't concern himself with that. He needed this dream to make sense.

"How could you send so many good people to hell, mister, and let a prostitute into heaven?"

"Why would you hold her past against her when I have already forgiven her?"

"Once a prostitute, always a prostitute."

"Do you really believe that?"

"Of course."

"Let's take a look at your life, Michael. You have made some choices that aren't much different from hers."

"I never sold my body for money."

"Maybe not for money, Michael."

"And how come you seem so familiar with my name. That's right, this is a dream so anything can happen. No matter how wacko. Let's take a look at my book. Might as well."

"Yes, let's. You have waited long enough, so let us begin."

He looked at Michael's book for a long time. "I guess you enjoyed your life for what it was Michael. Second Timothy two verse twenty two, People will be lovers of themselves, lovers of money, boastful, proud, abusive, disobedient to parents, ungrateful, unholy, without love, unforgiving, slanderous, without self-control, brutal, not lovers of good, treacherous, rash, conceited, lovers of pleasure rather than lovers of God....Does that summarize your fun filled life, Michael?"

Michael searched for a response and came up empty. That did kind of sum things up. But the man kept talking.

"That's the first time since you came to this room you have failed to give a response and here I thought you had an answer to everything. Let's take a look at your file of unforgiven sin."

The man opened Michael's book.

"A little over two hundred thousand," he said. "Pride, malice, disobedience, sexual immorality, lust, adultery, theft, lies, deception...this list is really long. You told your first lie when you were three. Your lifetime average for lying is thirteen per day."

"I have money, if it's money you want."

"Yes, I know you have money, Michael. You told lies so the innocent would be punished and the guilty would go free. You had the respect and adoration of all your peers. That must have felt really good....but why would I need your money when the cattle on a thousand hills belong to me? Your money and fame has no value here."

"What do you want?"

"Did you know that I paid the price for your redemption? You never accepted my gift did you. Did you know your mother prayed Ten Thousand, Six Hundred and Fourteen prayers for you from the day you were born?"

"I can't believe this is really happening."

"Still in denial, Michael?"

"This is not real."

"Your mother had forty seven conversations with you about me. That is a whole lot more than what most people get, and never once did you even consider me."

"About you? So, you're saying you are Jesus?"

Michael smiled. This dream really was getting weird.

"John 12:48," the Man quoted. "There is a judge for the one who rejects me and does not accept my words; that very word which I spoke will condemn him at the last day."

Michael played along. "I had all intention to go to church, eventually."

"The road to hell is paved with good intentions."

"You are sending me to hell?" A nervous laugh bubbled up from Michael's stomach.

"Hell is where you stored up your treasures, Michael, but it was your choice, not mine. I did offer you an alternative."

"You call that an alternative. It was ridiculously hard to accept."

He held up his hands to reveal the nail scars. "Harder than being nailed to a cross for people who would willfully continue to drive nails in my body with their sin for over two thousand years?"

The scars seemed more real than anything else he had seen since they had come to the room. Realization hit him like a speeding train.

"No more chances, Michael O'Connell."

The Man's facial expressed changed. For the briefest of seconds, he looked like Michael's mother, telling him that he might not get another chance.

Forty-seven chances.

Michael fell to his knees before the man. "Jesus."

"Your eyes have been opened, finally."

That was an understatement, Michael thought. He was truly dead and here before him stood the Son of God.

"Jesus, please spare me. I see you with my own eyes now. That's all I wanted to believe. I know the truth now and I am willing to change. I will do anything you say."

"There is no repentance in the grave."

"I see you now. I believe you now. Just give me another chance."

Forty-seven chances.

The words echoed in his soul.

"You had to believe without seeing, Michael. It's called faith. Your mother was a wonderful example."

"I needed more than faith."

"No you didn't."

"I don't want to go to hell. What kind of God are you to condemn people to such a terrible place?"

"I did everything I could to save you from it, Michael, but the final decision had always been yours."

"This is insane!"

Michael knew he was turning into a blubbering idiot like Marlon, but he didn't care. He didn't want to end up like his old friend Paul. He had clawed his way to the top of the law profession, far above anything Paul had ever established. He hadn't killed anybody. Or raped anybody. He was a good person, in his own mind.

And even though he had planned on spending two weeks in paradise with another man's wife, he hadn't actually done it.

"I am not a bad person," he pleaded. "I don't deserve hell."

"Do not be deceived. God cannot be mocked. Whatever a man sows that he will also reap."

"Give me one more chance. Please!"

"You had forty seven chances. Depart from me, you worker of iniquity. I do not know you."

Forty-seven chances.

As hell's jailers came to chain him and drag him away, Michael's mind replayed each and every conversation he ever had with his mother.

Forty-seven chances to escape the waiting room. Forty-seven chances to escape hell's torments. And he had not taken one of them.

Now, he had an eternity to remember each moment, each chance, in great detail.

Eternity is a long time to endure such torment, he thought. But even in that moment his mind could not fathom just how long eternity will be.

Don't miss out!

Visit the website below and you can sign up to receive emails whenever C.Orville McLeish publishes a new book. There's no charge and no obligation.

https://books2read.com/r/B-A-GABRB-DPHRD

BOOKS 2 READ

Connecting independent readers to independent writers.

Also by C.Orville McLeish

Christian Youth Faith-Walkers Series
Detour: A Christian Novel
The Preacha And The Prostitute: A Christian Novel
Agents of Christ: The Prodigal Daughter: A Christian Novel
Chains: A Christian Novel
The Waiting Room: A Christian Novel

The Unshakable Series
FAITH: A Theological Memoir

Standalone
Girl Unknown
Who I Am In Christ Daily Devotionals
How to Receive Your Healing
Sons of God:A Study on the Biblical Narrative of the Sons of
God
Made in God's Image: We are Partakers of God's Divine Nature

About the Author

C. Orville McLeish is a successful entrepreneur, and an acclaimed multi-award-winning author, playwright, and screenwriter. He is a professional ghostwriter, copy editor and self-publishing service provider. With a deep commitment to intellectual and mystical theology, he intertwines his passion for health, fitness, longevity, and Christian spirituality. A proud graduate of Writer's Digest University and the School of Kingdom Ministries, Cleveland is currently pursuing a master's in theological studies at Gordon-Conwell Theological Seminary.

Read more at https://clevelandomcleish.com/.

www.ingramcontent.com/pod-product-compliance
Lightning Source LLC
Chambersburg PA
CBHW060455160726
47992CB00003B/1222